# Too Much Rain

by Fran Manushkin

illustrated by Tammie Lyon

**Picture Window Books**
Minneapolis, Minnesota

Katie Woo is published by Picture Window Books
1710 Roe Crest Drive,
North Mankato, MN 56003
www.picturewindowbooks.com

Text © 2010 Fran Manushkin
Illustrations © 2010 Picture Window Books

Library of Congress Cataloging-in-Publication Data
Manushkin, Fran.
    Too much rain / by Fran Manushkin ; illustrated by Tammie Lyon.
    p. cm. — (Katie Woo)
    ISBN 978-1-4048-5494-9 (library binding)
    [1. Floods—Fiction. 2. Chinese Americans—Fiction.] I. Lyon, Tammie, ill. II. Title.
PZ7.M3195Tr 2010
[E]—dc22                                                        2009002191

Summary: When heavy rain causes flooding, Katie Woo and her parents spend the
night in a shelter.

Creative Director: Heather Kindseth
Graphic Designer: Emily Harris


Photo Credits
Fran Manushkin, pg. 26
Tammie Lyon, pg. 26

022017
010277R

Printed in the United States of America, North Mankato, Minnesota.

# Table of Contents

## Chapter 1
# Rain!

One day it started to
rain. It rained all day, and it
rained all night.

"When will it stop?" Katie
Woo asked her mom.

Katie's mom told her, "The weatherman says it will keep raining until tomorrow."

The mayor was on TV.

"There may be some

flooding," he warned.

"Everyone should go to a

shelter. When the rain stops,

you can go home."

Katie packed a suitcase

with shirts and pants and

underpants and pajamas.

She also took her teddy

bear and her cat Sweet Pea's

bowl and mouse toy.

"I want to take along our family photo album," said Katie's mom. "It  has all the pictures of us with Grandma and Grandpa. I thought it was in the living room. But I can't find it."

Katie helped search for the
album. But nobody found it.
The family had to leave
without it.

# Chapter 2

# The Shelter

As they drove away,

Katie saw water flooding

into her neighbors' houses.

It was scary!

The shelter was in the

high school gym.

Katie's friends Pedro and

JoJo were already there.

JoJo was holding her little

cat, Niblet.

"Niblet was hiding in the

closet," JoJo said. "We almost

had to leave without her."

That night, Katie slept on
a cot at the shelter. Many
other people did too.

The shelter felt strange to
Katie. She hugged Sweet Pea
and her teddy

bear tight.

The next morning, the mayor said, "I have good news! The rain has stopped. Everyone can go home."

Katie Woo was worried
about her house. Would it be
flooded with water?

# Chapter 3
# Going Home

Katie's family hurried

back to their house.

When they reached their

block, Katie saw her house

standing tall!

A stream of water was
pouring out of the basement
window.

Katie spotted something
floating in the water.

"Mom!" Katie shouted.

"It's our photo album!"

Katie's mom hurried out

of the car and grabbed the

album before it floated away.

"The cover is wet, but

the pages are okay,"

she said.

The family was so happy
to be home!

They made hot chocolate
and drank it in their warm
kitchen.

"There is some water in the basement," said Katie's dad. "But we can pump it out."

Katie called her friends JoJo and Pedro. Their houses were safe too.

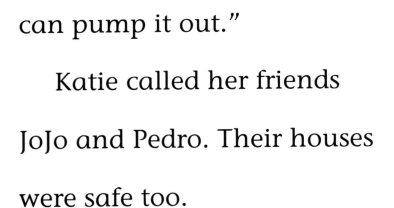

"We were lucky," said
Katie's mom. "We have our
house, and we have each
other."

"Let's take a happy picture for our photo album," Katie said.

So they did!

## About the Author

Fran Manushkin is the author of many popular picture books, including *How Mama Brought the Spring; Baby, Come Out!; Latkes and Applesauce: A Hanukkah Story;* and *The Tushy Book.* There is a real Katie Woo — she's Fran's great-niece — but she never gets in half the trouble of the Katie Woo in the books. Fran writes on her beloved Mac computer in New York City, without the help of her two naughty cats, Cookie and Goldy.

## About the Illustrator

Tammie Lyon began her love for drawing at a young age while sitting at the kitchen table with her dad. She continued her love of art and eventually attended the Columbus College of Art and Design, where she earned a bachelors degree in fine art. After a brief career as a professional ballet dancer, she decided to devote herself full time to illustration. Today she lives with her husband, Lee, in Cincinnati, Ohio. Her dogs, Gus and Dudley, keep her company as she works in her studio.

# Glossary

**basement** (BAYSS-muhnt)—an area in a building that is below ground level

**kitchen** (KICH-uhn)—a room in which food is prepared and cooked

**photos** (FOH-tohz)—pictures taken by a camera

**shelter** (SHEL-tur)—a place where you are safe during bad weather

**worried** (WUR-eed)—felt uneasy about something

 Discussion Questions

1. The flooding was scary for Katie Woo. Have you ever been scared by bad weather? What happened?

2. Why was the photo album so important to Katie's family?

3. It felt strange to Katie to sleep in the gym. Have you ever slept someplace strange?

# Writing Prompts

1. Write a list of five words that describe a rainstorm.

2. The Woos' photo album had pictures of them with Katie's grandparents. Grandparents are special people. Write a sentence about what makes grandparents special.

3. Katie packed clothes, her bear, and some things for her cat. What would you pack if you needed to suddenly leave your home? Make a list.

# Having Fun with Katie Woo

In *Too Much Rain*, it rained so much that Katie Woo, her friends and her family all had to go to the shelter. Even though it usually doesn't rain enough to flood, rain can still ruin your day. But it doesn't have to!

Here is a fun indoor game that can be played rain or shine. Just be sure you have a grown-up's permission.

**The Super Taste Challenge**

**What you need:**

- a blindfold

- a variety of food (Don't forget to ask your grown-up if anything in the kitchen is off limits.)

## What you do:

1. Choose one person to take the Super Taste Challenge, and cover his or her eyes with the blindfold.

2. The other players select a food to give the taster. The taster should think, *Is it sour, sweet, spicy? Is it crunchy or soft?* Then the taster guesses what the food is. If the guess is right, it is someone else's turn to taste. If it is wrong, try another food.

Here are a few good foods to try:

- pickles
- crackers
- salad dressing
- mustard
- apples
- tomato sauce
- olives
- raisins
- carrots